Everybody loves a scary story. Now you can enjoy tales that
come with a good dose of fright, lots of suspense and a bit of
humour too! Phobia books are about all your favourite spooky
subjects such as monster aliens, haunted houses, scary dolls
and magical powers that go haywire.

Read on if you dare!

SPECTROPHOBIA

THE FEAR OF MIRRORS

EVERYONE IS AFRAID OF SOMETHING.

You might be afraid of quite a number of things. But a **PHOBIA** is a very special fear. It is deep and strong and long-lasting. It is hard to explain why people have phobias — sometimes they seem to come out of nowhere.

Anders, a boy who is haunted by mirrors, does indeed learn their secrets. But even after reading the last chapter, you might wonder if he is too late.

Do you think it's cool to write a secret message backwards on a sheet of paper, and then read it correctly in a mirror's reflection? You might not after reading this story. Read on to find out why. . .

1

At first there were only small differences in my bathroom mirror. The angle of my toothpaste tube, the way the toilet paper was hanging. But there was always something that didn't match the actual bathroom, like a spot-the-difference game. It had been going on all week.

Things got even more eerie this morning. The mirror targeted my lucky top. It was a blue polo with a deer logo on it. After I washed my face, I peered up at my reflection in the bathroom mirror. The deer icon was gone. The shirt was plain blue.

When I looked down at my chest, though, the deer was there.

I peered in the mirror again and noticed the clock on the wall behind me behaving strangely. Its hands were spinning wildly. Then they stopped. I turned around to look at the real clock. The second hand was moving along in its usual rhythm. I spun back to the mirror and gazed at the frozen clock, waiting for something to happen. Within moments, the clock in the mirror dropped to the floor and shattered without a sound.

I let out a shriek and glanced behind me to see if the real clock had fallen. It still hung on the wall. In a panic, I ran downstairs to the kitchen.

"Mum, Dad!" I yelled. "Something's wrong with the bathroom mirror!"

My parents stared blankly at me, then turned to each other. My dad shrugged.

"What do you mean?" asked my mum, turning back to me.

"It's showing things that aren't real," I blurted out. After I'd said the words, I realized how strange it must have sounded. My parents' faces changed from confused to annoyed.

"Stop playing games, Anders," said Dad. "It's getting late. You'd better hurry up and get ready. I don't want to have to drive you in if you miss the bus."

Of course they thought I was making it up. I hardly believed it myself. But then I saw movement on the fridge's shiny surface. It was a reflection of the kitchen clock. Its hands were moving so quickly, they looked like tiny propellers.

Without a word, I ran back upstairs to my bedroom. I flopped onto my bed face down and tried to wrap my head around what I was seeing. Could I be imagining all of it?

I heard noises in the room next to mine. My sister, Jennie, was stirring in her bedroom. If I didn't get up and into the bathroom now, she would purposely take her time just to get on my nerves.

I darted into the bathroom and swung the door shut just as my sister opened hers. Heavy footsteps plodded across the landing. Then came three solid knocks on the door.

"Anders, you did that just because you knew I wanted to go in there!" she cried.

"What are big brothers for?" I said.

With a dramatic sigh, Jennie stomped back to her bedroom and slammed the door. I chuckled. It was so easy to annoy her. But the smile slid off my face as I stared into the mirror again.

I planted both my hands on the sink and narrowed my eyes. I scanned the entire mirror from left to right, from top to bottom and then I did it again. I couldn't find a single thing that was different between the bathroom and the reflection.

I stared at my confused face in the mirror, wondering if it was just my imagination. Then the reflection showed my hand turning on the tap.

Water gushed out faster than it could drain down the sink. It splashed onto the floor. But I hadn't moved my hands. My eyes shot down towards the tap. It wasn't on. I frowned, confused.

When I looked up at my reflection, it was smiling.

2

Terrified by what I'd seen in the mirror, I
rushed back to my room and slammed the door.
Beads of sweat were forming on my forehead.
I closed my eyes and took a deep breath. I
convinced myself that I didn't need to brush
my teeth or wash my face. Instead, I threw
on the jeans I'd worn yesterday and grabbed
my backpack, coat, hat and gloves. I headed
downstairs, waved goodbye to my parents, and
waited outside for the bus.

When I saw the bus coming down the street,

I made my way to the kerb. I kept my head down. I didn't know if the weird sightings would show up in other reflections too, and I didn't want to find out now. The brakes screeched as the bus came to a stop. The doors whooshed open. I kept my eyes down as I hoisted myself up the steps and found an empty seat.

I sat and stared at my backpack. I was afraid to catch my reflection in the window. Even when my best friend Curt flopped down next to me, my eyes didn't budge.

"Hey, Anders," he said. "Is there something magical about that backpack I should know about? You're staring it down like it's the last piece of cake in the shop."

"Yeah, it does my homework for me," I joked. "I just have to watch to make sure it keeps working."

Curt chuckled. But when I still didn't look at him, he tried again. "I won't turn you to stone like Medusa."

This time I let out a snort. I turned to Curt and focused on his face.

"Wow!" he exclaimed. "I broke the trance!" He held out his hand. We had created a secret handshake when we were in primary school. It was silly, but we couldn't kick the habit. I grabbed his hand, and we went through our routine.

"So what's up?" asked Curt. "You seem distracted, even for a Friday."

"I've . . . been seeing things," I said. "It started when . . ." I trailed off. How could I explain it to Curt? My parents thought I was making it all up. He probably would too.

Curt piped up, as if reading my mind. "Try me, Anders. I promise I won't laugh."

I sighed. "There's something wrong with . . . mirrors."

Immediately, the left side of his lip started to quiver. It looked like he was about to laugh.

I raised my eyebrows at him, and he got his lip under control.

"Reflections aren't the same as real life," I continued. "They're close, but they're not the same."

Curt thought about it for a moment. "Can you give me an example?"

"Well, one morning a few weeks ago, I pulled the shower curtain completely shut after stepping out. But in the mirror, it was halfway open. Or the hand towel last weekend. I threw it on the side after using it. But in the mirror, it was neatly folded."

Curt said, "I know you wouldn't lie to me. But what you describe doesn't seem possible. You know?"

My shoulders slumped. Even my best friend didn't believe me.

Curt was going to say something else, I think, but instead he punched me on the arm.

"Hey, it's pizza day for lunch. Pizza makes everything better."

I couldn't help but smile. But as I looked at his face, I saw movement in the window behind him. My reflected face tilted to the side and peered back at me from around Curt's head.

3

I've always been good at school. I get mostly As and Bs, and I can usually answer the question if the teacher asks me. Or I can at least fake my way through an answer. But this morning, I couldn't concentrate on anything except what I'd seen in the reflections.

With my eyes barely open and aimed at the ground, it took me a while to find my seat in science. Large mirrors hung around the room so they could be pulled down as needed. They were supposed to help with some of our lab work on light and physics. We hadn't used them yet.

With so many shiny mirrors hanging all around me, the rest of the world faded out of my mind, even as the lesson began.

"Anders? Would you care to take a guess?"

I jumped at my name and realized I hadn't heard a word Mr Romberg had said.

"Sorry, Mr Romberg. Could you repeat the question?" I asked.

The teacher's head tilted downwards. He peered at me over his glasses. I swore I could see shadows moving in the reflection of the glasses' lenses.

"My question was simple, Anders," Mr Romberg said. "I asked you what day it was. Of course, that was after I asked you what the definition of a prism is. As you didn't answer, I thought you'd like an easier question."

I sank into my chair as Mr Romberg continued to embarrass me in front of the whole class. My eyes shifted to the line of mirrors behind him.

The mixture of light and shadows from the mirrors seemed to vibrate. The longer I gazed at the mirrors, the faster the vibrations moved. Before long, the light and shadows combined into a dark grey ripple, pulsing rapidly from the centre.

"Anders!" cried Mr Romberg. "If you can't pay attention, you can remove yourself from my classroom. Please go to the Head's office."

I snatched my textbook and notebook from my desk. With my free hand, I reached down for my pencil. I was shaking so badly, I knocked the pencil to the floor. In my hurry to leave, I accidentally kicked the pencil and sent it skittering to the front of the room and under a desk. A few of my classmates sniggered as I got on all fours to chase it down. Mr Romberg sighed loudly. I finally snatched the pencil and ran out of the room. Even a trip to the head teacher's office seemed ten times better than staying in that room, surrounded by crazy mirrors.

4

My friends and I claimed a corner table at lunch. They were eager to hear how my meeting with Headmistress Lewin had gone.

"It was nothing," I said. "She lectured me about the importance of paying attention and getting a good education. I nodded at everything she said. And it was over. It was the first time I'd been called to her office, so I got off easy."

Curt sat back. He was clearly disappointed by the lack of drama.

"You spaced out big-time," said Trevor.

"Even I know what a prism is."

"Thanks," I said. "I appreciate the support."

"I know Mr Romberg has a temper," said Dan, "but you were pretty much ignoring him."

My pizza sat untouched on my tray. The cheese was beginning to cool and harden. I poked at it with my fork. Just then, the room lit up from a lightning strike outside. Another autumn storm. Just what I needed for my walk home.

"Tell them about the mirrors," said Curt.

I shot him a nasty look. "It's not a big deal," I said. "Mirrors are freaking me out a bit. I think I'm just tired."

A deep chuckle rose from the table next to us.

"Yeah, man, mirrors are terrifying," said Duke with an annoying grin. Duke was the biggest boy at school. As well as being bigger than the rest of us, he also had a bad temper. Everyone knew it was best to stay off his radar. I kept quiet, hoping he'd lose interest.

"Back off, Duke," said Trevor. "You're just mad because mirrors break when you look at them."

Duke and his friends stood up abruptly from their table and glared at us. They started to walk towards us. Just then, Mr Duncan, the football coach, slammed through the doors. He stomped towards Duke with a scowl on his face.

"Whitlock! Why weren't you at practice yesterday?" asked Mr Duncan. "Our first game is tonight! That was the third practice you've missed this week!"

Duke stammered out a reply. We took our chance to escape. We dropped off our trays and slid past the coach towards the doors. I glanced back at Duke and immediately wished I hadn't. His angry glare told me this encounter wasn't over.

5

The storm had cleared by the time school finished. Curt and I walked home in silence as I thought about the incident with Duke. I wasn't as scared of him as I normally would be. Whatever was happening with the mirrors was soaking up all the fear my mind could take.

Curt piped up. "You know, I doubt Duke and his friends will beat us up. They'd get suspended and miss the rest of the football season."

"Nah," I said. "He'll wait until the end of the season. Then he won't care if he gets suspended."

"Hmmm. Good point," said Curt. "At least you won't get beaten up on the walk home! But you might get wet. . . ."

He jumped in a puddle next to me. The water sloshed over my legs, soaking my feet up to my ankles. I swung my foot at another nearby puddle like I was kicking a football. The small wave drenched the front of Curt's jeans. We laughed.

I looked down at the puddle I'd just kicked, watching the water settle and become still. I realized too late that I was again staring at my reflection. It smiled at me with an open mouth. Its teeth were pointed. Saliva oozed over its lips. A long, narrow tongue slid out of its mouth. I couldn't look away.

Was I losing my mind?

Suddenly, water shot up like a geyser from a puddle behind Curt. Another puddle spewed up, then sloshed to the ground. Like tiny fountains, all of the puddles around us shot water into the air. The streams created a watery prison around us.

Then, all at once, the streams of water came crashing to the ground. When they'd settled, they had formed a giant puddle around us.

"Did you see it, Curt?" I asked, wiping water from my brow. "Did you see my reflection in the water?"

Curt just looked at me. His eyes moved from my face to the puddle and back again. Then he looked away, unable to hold my stare.

"I've gotta get going," he said finally. "I'll talk to you later."

I wondered why Curt wouldn't answer me. Still, I reached out to him to do our secret handshake. "OK, man," I said. But Curt didn't take my hand. Instead he hoisted his backpack onto his shoulders and walked ahead without me.

6

As if the day's events weren't bad enough, I remembered that my mum planned to take me clothes shopping after school. I went to my room to change out of my wet clothes, dreading the task ahead.

My mum was already waiting for me in the garage. She was talking to someone on her Bluetooth as she slid into the driver's seat. I was glad she was distracted and wouldn't want to talk. I got into the passenger's seat, careful to avoid looking at the side mirror. As we passed the first car on the street, I saw my monstrous reflection in the driver's side window. I clamped my eyes shut for the rest of the drive.

When we got to the shops, I kept my eyes focused on my shoelaces. My mum, still on her Bluetooth, didn't even seem to notice.

Once we entered T.J.Maxx, she grabbed a basket and immediately started pulling clothes off the nearest rail. She inspected each one as if she was a crime scene investigator. After analysing what seemed like three hundred tops, she got off her Bluetooth and handed ten tops to me.

"Oh, no," she said when I didn't budge. "We do this every time. I pick out clothes for you. You refuse to try them on. Then I end up returning at least half of what I bought. The fitting rooms are over there." She pointed to the back corner of the shop.

It was a battle I wouldn't win. I started walking, but as I drew closer to the fitting rooms, my arms began to shake. The tops felt like they weighed a tonne. Every step closer to the fitting rooms – and the mirrors – made my heart beat faster.

I froze as soon as I reached the entrance. But I told myself that if I kept my back to the mirror, I'd be fine. At least that's what I hoped.

I shuffled into the first cubicle, eyes down. I promptly turned my back to the wall with the mirror. I took off the top I was wearing and reached for the first in the pile. Yellow? I hate the colour yellow.

Scritch. Scritch. Scritch. Scritch.

The noise was coming from behind me. From the mirror.

Scritch. Scritch. Scritch. Scritch.

I wasn't going to hang around to see what was making the sound.

I looked for the top I had been wearing. It was lying underneath the mirror. As I quickly grabbed it, I caught a glimpse of my reflection. I couldn't

help but stare at the terrifying scene unfolding in the mirror.

Long nails on the right hand of my reflection thrummed against the glass. The four fingers moved against the glass impatiently while the thumb rested on the mirror's edge. The sky blue colour of my eyes changed in the reflection to pitch black. Dark shapes like black worms slithered outwards and covered the whites of the creature's eyes. Only black pits remained.

The sound stopped.

The reflection raised its left hand. It pointed at me. The finger extended, then curled, over and over again. It was beckoning me to come closer. A sharp-toothed smile stretched across the monster's face.

Behind the hideous creature, the walls of the fitting room began cracking and peeling. Paint chips fell from the walls. Suddenly, the pile of tops erupted in flames. I could feel the heat from the fire. I could smell the smoke. But when I spun around to look at the actual fitting room, everything was normal. When I looked back at the reflection, everything had returned to normal there as well. My head was throbbing. Was my mind playing tricks on me? Was this all in my imagination?

In an instant, my reflection opened its mouth in rage. The creature had returned. It charged the mirror and pounded it with its fist. Cracks resembling a spider's web spread from the point of impact. I stumbled backwards, scrambling for the lock on the door. I felt tears rolling down my face as I bolted out of the fitting room.

7

I wiped the tears from my face as I ran. I was halfway across the shop before I realized I didn't have my top on. It was still clutched tight in my fist. I pulled it over my head and breathed deep, trying to slow my racing heart.

My mum and I had a huge argument in the car on the way home. But I don't even remember what she was saying. When she pulled into our driveway, I started to shake again. Obviously I couldn't avoid mirrors forever. I got out of the car and stood motionless on the front lawn.

Mum walked into the house, the door banging behind her.

Scritch. Scritch. Scritch.

Even out here I could hear the faint scratching from the bathroom. I couldn't go into the house. I had to get away. I got out my phone and called Trevor.

"Hey, Trevor," I said. My voice was shaky. "Do you want to head over to the county fair?"

"Hotdogs!" he yelled before hanging up. I suppose that was a yes.

I called Dan, too, who was eager to join us. I thought about texting Curt. But I stopped before hitting "send". I still felt weird about what had happened earlier.

Scritchscritchscritchscritch.

The scratching echoed once again. This time it was at a quicker pace.

I heard Mum open the front door behind me. She yelled something.

I didn't reply. I was already running down the street.

The fairground wasn't far from my house, but I was glad I was still wearing my coat, jacket and gloves. It was really cold for early autumn. Still, I was glad to be out of the house.

I found Dan and Trevor squaring off in a game where you shoot water out of a pistol at a target. Trevor won and chose a toy penguin as his prize. As we walked through the fair, Trevor danced the penguin in front of Dan's face, taunting him.

We stopped at a food van selling hotdogs. Then, as we ate, we walked through the fair. We passed countless food vans and stalls selling sunglasses, jewellery and antiques.

"Look at that," said Dan. He pointed across the fair. "It's an old-fashioned funhouse."

We walked over to the carnival attraction. It was decorated with wild animals and creepy clowns. Paint was peeling in several places, and graffiti covered much of the artwork.

"Do you have what it takes to make it through the world's most complex funhouse?" said Trevor in a booming voice, reading from the sign next to the entrance. The sign detailed the obstacles we would find in the funhouse. Rotating walls, spinning rooms, trick doors.

"What do you think?" asked Dan. "Should we give it a try?"

"You guys go ahead," I said. "I'm going to grab another hotdog."

"Are you still freaking out about the mirrors?" asked Trevor.

"Yeah, what's wrong with mirrors?" someone said from behind me. A second later, I felt a rough shove. It was Duke Whitlock.

"Know what Coach tells us?" he said. "The only way to conquer your fear is to face it. And because I'm such a nice guy, this one's on me."

He reached into his pocket and pulled out a wad of tickets. He thrust them towards the attendant.

"Go on!" taunted Duke. "Face your fears!" His friends laughed and egged him on as he pushed me into the entrance of the funhouse.

8

Duke stood at the entrance. His huge body practically shut out the light. Behind him, Duke's friends were holding back Trevor and Dan. There was no way my friends could break through and get to me.

"Get out of here!" I shouted. "Just leave me alone!"

I heard the attendant's voice. "Hey, what's going on? Are you boys OK?" he said.

Duke leaned out of the door and smiled at the attendant. "Everything's good here," he said. "It's a class initiation." He laughed.

Then Duke stared me down. "Do it!" he said in a loud whisper. He shoved me again. Hard. So hard, in fact, that he stumbled forward himself. He quickly regained his balance and lurched back towards the entrance. It was almost as if he was afraid of the funhouse himself.

I braced myself against a wall and focused on slowing my breathing. Duke pointed down the dark entrance. After a minute, I pulled it together and took my first few steps. It was just a silly carnival attraction, after all.

The first room was large and covered in swirling patterns. The floor was one giant spinning disc. I hopped onto the disc and scurried to the middle to get my bearings. I scanned the walls, looking for a way out. My eyes settled on a narrow opening between two spinning wheels. I took small, shuffling steps towards the edge of the spinning disc. Then I waited for the narrow doorway to reach me.

I jumped through the opening and immediately tumbled to the floor. I was in a long, rotating tunnel. I scrambled through the tunnel on my hands and knees before emerging into a room with flashing lights. The floor was lined with oversized tiles that shot up and down at random. I stumbled a few times but cleared the obstacles quickly. After leaving that room, I was met with a large sign: *The World's Greatest Mirror Maze.*

I was going to have to make my way through the maze with my eyes closed. I couldn't stand to look at the creature again. I thought of advice my dad had given me when I once got lost in a maze. When he finally found me, he'd said, "When in doubt, always go left. If you reach a dead end, go back and keep going left whenever you can. Eventually, you'll find your way out." That's what I planned to do now.

I squeezed my eyes shut and reached out to my left. My glove hit the smooth surface of a mirror. I kept my left hand on the mirror. Then I slowly worked my way forward.

Scritch. Scritch. Scritch. Scritch.

I jolted away from the scratching sound, my back hitting a wall. I stood still, my mind racing. Then there were more scratches behind me. Then in front of me, and again behind me. Soon, the scritch-scritch-scritching of the creature's hideous nails echoed throughout the maze.

The creature had me surrounded.

I panicked and reached out, feeling for any gaps I could find in the mirrors. Every path I took was met with more scratching. I banged roughly into a mirror every few seconds. Then I ran shoulder-first into something softer.

"Oof! Watch where you're going."

I opened my eyes. It was Duke, standing at the exit with two of his friends behind him. Now he was blocking my escape.

Duke spun me around and shoved me back into the funhouse. I was facing the mirrors again. This time, with my eyes wide open. Everything I saw was multiplied. Reflections of reflections of reflections. My breath caught in my throat. Hundreds of narrowed eyes stared back at me from the mirrors.

9

The creature in the funhouse mirrors
extended its finger and motioned me to come
closer. But this time its nails were longer,
and they were growing. Within seconds, the
creature's nails had grown impossibly long. The
nails curled as they grew. The tips were as sharp
as knives.

The mirrors pulsed like they had in the
science classroom. Shadows fell on the creature's
face. Soon only its beady black eyes stared at me.

I heard Duke gasp. I slumped to the ground and scooted backwards on my hands and knees. Suddenly I fell through the funhouse exit, slid down a smooth chute and landed roughly in the dirt. Duke's friends gathered around me, pointing and laughing.

"You should have seen his buddies run away," one of them said with a smirk. "A pair of real wimps."

"Back off!" yelled Duke. He jumped down from the funhouse. His friends were silent.

One of Duke's friends spoke up. "Hey, man, you're the one—"

"Well now I'm telling you to lay off!" Duke shouted.

With confused looks on their faces, Duke's friends stumbled off through the fair. Then Duke turned to me. "I get why you're afraid of . . ." he trailed off. "I've seen it too. And I don't mean just in there. I first saw it in the cafeteria, after Coach told me off. It freaked me out. I was a coward.

I was hoping by forcing you to confront the monster, I wouldn't have to. I'm so sorry."

"You know it's real," I said. The look in Duke's eyes made me even more afraid. Our nightmares were coming true.

Duke held out his hand. I paused for a moment before grasping it.

"Hey, Duke! Leave him alone!" said a familiar voice behind me. It was Curt.

"He was helping me up," I said. Curt had a look of disbelief on his face. "What are you doing here?" I asked.

"Dan called me after he got off the phone with you," Curt said. "Sorry, bud. What I saw in those puddles freaked me out. I took off when you needed me the most. I thought the monster was only after you, so I ran. When I got home, the monster was there waiting for me."

"We're not the only ones who've seen it," I said. Then I glanced over at Duke.

Curt understood. He must have thought that anything that would make Duke friendly had to be big. It had to be pretty horrifying, in fact.

"So, what's the plan?" asked Curt.

"Plan?" I said blankly.

"We've got to get rid of that . . . thing," said Duke. "There's three of us, and only one of him."

"Right," said Curt. "So where do we start?"

"Start?" I thought about it for a second. "We go to the place where this all began. My house," I said, even though it was the last place I wanted to go.

In complete silence, we walked to my house. Once inside, I found a note on the kitchen table. My mum and sister had gone to the cinema and Dad was out food shopping. That was probably for the best.

Curt, Duke and I climbed the stairs and entered the bathroom. With Curt on my left and

Duke on my right, the three of us stared into the mirror. I could feel Curt slightly shaking. Duke was breathing hard.

Seconds ticked by, then minutes. The only movement was our eyes scanning the mirror or shuffling from one foot to the other.

"Is that it?" asked Duke. "It's just gone?"

It didn't make sense. Why had I been tormented by this creature? Why wasn't it appearing now? What did it want?

Then it hit me.

"It only wants me," I said. "It won't show itself while you're here."

"It did before," said Curt. "Why wouldn't it now?"

"I don't know," I replied. "But nothing's happening. Wait outside the door. Let's see if I can draw the creature out."

Curt rested his arm against the towel rail and looked at Duke hesitantly. Duke shrugged and

Then my reflection let out an inhuman laugh. A mixture of fear and anger washed over me.

"What did you do?" I cried.

".won uoy m'I" the creature said. The sound was a collection of voices. It sounded both male and female, both deep and high-pitched. It sounded like it was echoing from within a deep well. But what was it saying?

The creature stepped forward. It breathed heavily onto the mirror, creating a small area of fogged glass. With a single finger, it wrote the words "I'm you now."

I stared at the words blankly. "What do you mean?"

The creature's head darted back and forth while it kept its eyes on me. ".uoy htcaW .uoy cimiM .uoy emoceB"

I shook my head, not able to understand.

The creature breathed onto the mirror again and wrote, "Watch you. Mimic you. Become you."

"How can you be me? You're in a mirror!"

The creature waved its hand through the air. Then it gave a quick snap of its wrist. The hands of the clock on my side of the mirror began spinning. I felt sick to my stomach. We must have swapped places when I placed my hand on the mirror. I must be in another dimension – or worse.

Then came a knock on the door. Curt's voice rang through from the other side. "Are you OK, Anders?"

The creature waved its hand again. A shadow fell over the mirror. It breathed on the mirror one last time and wrote, "No one will find you."

The creature turned away from me and opened the bathroom door. As it stepped into the corridor, I banged against the mirror wildly, trying to get my friends' attention. They didn't even flinch.

"We thought we heard something," Duke said. "Were you talking to it?"

"That thing wouldn't show itself," the demon replied in my voice. "I was trying to trick it out of hiding. But it didn't work. It must really be gone."

"That's great!" said Curt. "Hopefully that's the end of it, then. Let's go and meet up with Dan and Trevor and try to forget about this whole thing."

Curt then held out his hand towards the creature. The secret handshake! Maybe the creature didn't know about it!

My hopes were quickly dashed as the creature reached out and took Curt's hand. They went through the motions of the secret handshake, which ended with Curt's left hand firmly holding the creature's left hand.

"NOW!" shouted Curt.

Duke rushed up from behind and used his

forearm to pin the creature against the wall. He took the creature's right arm and wrenched it upwards so it couldn't move.

"Ow!" cried the creature. "What are you guys doing?"

"You're not Anders!" yelled Curt. He grabbed the creature's shoulder tightly with his free hand, keeping its left hand firmly in his own. Together, Curt and Duke forced the creature towards the mirror.

It let out a throaty snarl. At the hideous sound, Duke loosened his grip for a moment. The creature tried to thrash free. Duke regained his grip and pushed forward.

When they reached the sink, Curt thrust the creature's hand against the mirror. Without hesitation, I thrust my palm against the mirror opposite the creature's hand.

Instantly, the room began to spin once again. I closed my eyes and waited for it to stop. I jerked my hand away from the mirror as soon as I could, knocking over Curt and Duke in the process.

Breathing heavily, I helped them off the floor. Duke pointed past me without saying a word.

I turned towards the mirror, eyeing my reflection. The creature was seething. Its eyes burrowed into each of us in turn. It lashed out, slamming its fist against the mirror. Cracks appeared. But with a crinkling sound, the cracks disappeared. The mirror was whole once again. Then the creature faded until only my true reflection remained.

"How did you know what to do?" I asked. Curt turned to the towel rail and picked up his phone.

"Duke FaceTimed me before we left the bathroom. I hid my phone here, and we heard and saw everything."

I threw my arms around Curt. Duke put a hand on my shoulder and smiled. I let out a sigh of relief. Now that I knew its secret, I was confident the creature would give up.

"Let's go to my place," said Curt. "You guys can help me break in my new PS4 game."

"As long as the game doesn't involve mirrors, I'm in," I said.

EPILOGUE

The house was dark.

Quiet.

Everyone was asleep except Jennie. She was leaving the bathroom when she heard a strange sound behind her.

Scritch. Scritch. Scritch. Scritch.

Was it coming from the mirror?

GLOSSARY

bearings getting used to your location, where you are

drenched made something completely wet

eerie strange and frightening

glimpse quick look

hideous ugly or horrible

hoisted lifted or pulled up

initiation bring someone into a club or group, usually by way of a special ceremony

mimic copy

piped suddenly spoke

plodded moved in a slow, heavy way

prism triangular piece of glass used to produce bands of coloured light

saliva clear liquid in your mouth that helps you swallow and begin to digest food

thrummed made a repeated humming or beating sound

FACE YOUR FEAR!

Now that you've read the story, it's no longer only inside this book. It's also in your brain. Can your brain help you answer the questions below?

1. Jennie hears sounds in the mirror at the end of the story. Write a chapter or short story about what happens to her next.

2. Write a secret message to a friend, and put it in the mirror language from Chapter 10.

3. If you were replaced with a mirror creature, how would your friends work out it wasn't the real you? Write down a list of ways they could tell.

4. Anders lets his fears about the mirror affect his schoolwork. Talk about a time when it was hard for you to focus on something. What were you thinking of instead? Something happy? Something sad? Something scary?

5. Duke turned out to be less of a bully and more of a friend. Were you surprised about that? What do you think made him stop behaving like a bully? Is there something in the story that tells you?

FEAR FACTORS

spectrophobia — the fear of mirrors

Magical mirrors feature in many famous stories.

In the tale of Snow White, the Evil Queen always asks her enchanted mirror who is the most beautiful in all the kingdom. One day, she gets a big surprise.

Harry Potter discovers the enchanted Mirror of Erised that reveals what people desire most in the world. "Erised" is "desire" spelled backwards.

Alice (of Wonderland fame) slips through a looking glass, or mirror, to enter a bizarre world laid out as a gigantic chessboard, where she meets Tweedledum and Tweedledee, Humpty Dumpty and the monstrous Jabberwocky.

"Bloody, Bloody Mary" is a creepy folklore legend. If you stare into a mirror in a dark room lit only by a candle, and say Bloody Mary's name several times, the mysterious woman's face will appear in the mirror.

Brain scientists agree that you might actually see Bloody Mary's face, or the face of an animal or some other creature in the mirror due to your brain's visual centre being confused by the dim, reflected image and sending out the wrong messages.

Do you think someone you know is a vampire? If they don't have a reflection in a mirror, they might be one of the undead!

Some people believe if you break a mirror you get seven years of bad luck. However, enslaved African American people who lived in the American South more than a hundred years ago believed you could undo the curse by washing the broken pieces of the mirror in a flowing river for seven hours.

ABOUT THE AUTHOR

Anthony Wacholtz is a writer and editor with a love of things that go bump in the night. He has been a horror fan ever since he was young. His favourite books cover everything from R.L. Stine's Goosebumps to the works of Stephen King. Anthony lives with his wife, son and dog in Minnesota, USA, where he is ready and waiting for the zombie apocalypse.

ABOUT THE ILLUSTRATOR

Mariano Epelbaum is a character designer, illustrator and traditional 2D animator. He has been working as a professional artist since 1996, and enjoys trying different art styles and techniques. Throughout his career Mariano has created characters and designs for a wide range of films, TV series, adverts and publications in his native country of Argentina. He has also contributed to several books for children, including Fairy Tale Mix-ups, You Choose: Fractured Fairy Tales and Snoops, Inc.

GRIMM AND GROSS

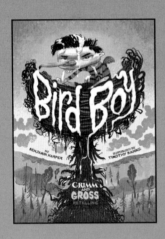

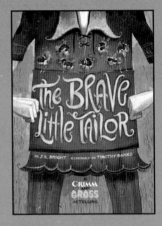

only from Raintree